ZiGGY FiNDS A HOME

WRitten & iLLUSTRATED BY
Amy NiCKERSON
FOR my zigzigs

Printed in the United States of America
First Printing, 2018
ISBN 978-0-692-19843-8

Wild Heart Publishing
2521 NW 12th St
Oklahoma City, OK 73107

wild heart
PUBLISHING

Ziggy didn't have a home like most dogs.
He lived on the street.
He spent his days bouncing around.

Ziggy loved to bounce, but all that
bouncing made his tummy very hungry.

He stuck his nose way up high.
There was a yummy smell in the air!
"I know that smell," Ziggy said.
"It's my favorite thing to eat!"

PiZZA!

Oh, the taste of a good slice of pizza!
Pepperoni. Sausage.
And all that ooey, gooey cheese.
Ziggy loved pizza!

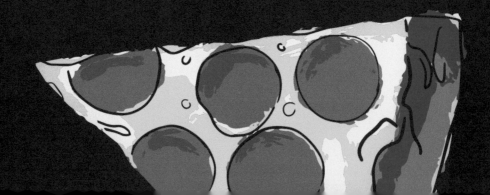

"That's the tastiest pizza I've ever smelled! But where's it coming from?" thought Ziggy.

Ziggy ran to check the trash cans nearby.
Maybe the pizza would be inside?
He opened up the lid and out popped a raccoon!

"Whatcha lookin' for?" the raccoon asked.
"Pizza! Do you have any?" Ziggy asked.
"Nope. No pizza. But, I did see a food truck in
the park. Maybe they have pizza?"
"Thanks!" Ziggy said.
"Good luck!" shouted the raccoon.

The park was very busy with people.
Some were sitting on benches.
Some were riding bikes.
Some were playing catch.
And some were standing in line at a big white truck.
"Maybe that's the truck with the pizza?"
Ziggy thought.

SNOW CONES

He ran over to the white truck.
By the side of the truck, he saw
a giant sign.

In big, bright letters it read
SNOW CONES.

There was no pizza at
this food truck.
Ziggy didn't know where
to look next!

As he left the park, a bird
landed in front of him.
Ziggy saw something hanging
from his mouth.
It was round and red.
It was a PEPPERONI!

"Where did you find that?" Ziggy asked.
"Oh this? I got it at the giant oak tree
down the street. A squirrel gave it to me."
"Thanks!" Ziggy said.
"You're welcome!" squeaked the bird.

Ziggy arrived at the giant oak tree.
It grew in front of a small gray house.
A squirrel came running down the tree.
He stopped right in front of Ziggy to
chomp on something.

"Is that pizza crust?"
Ziggy asked the squirrel.
"Yep. I got it from the lady in
the gray house.
She makes the best pizza!"
said the squirrel.
"Thanks!" Ziggy said.
"No problem!" said the squirrel.

Ziggy bounced up to the house.
He could smell the delicious scent
of freshly baked pizza coming
from the window.
His tummy started to growl.
He was so very hungry!

A lady opened the front door.
Ziggy ran up to her.

"Oh hi! Who are you, little guy?" asked the lady.
Ziggy sat at her feet and tilted his head.
"Aren't you sweet!" she said.
"You look kinda hungry. Why don't you come inside?
I just baked a fresh pepperoni pizza!"

The nice lady took Ziggy to the kitchen.
In no time he'd gobbled down several slices
of the tastiest pizza he'd ever had.

"You look a little lost, and you're such a
sweet puppy," said the lady. "I would love to
keep you if you don't have a home!"

After he ate, the lady gave him a bath.
"We'll get you cleaned up!" she said.
Ziggy wasn't a big fan of the water.
But he liked feeling clean!
He was glad someone loved and cared for him.

When they came out of the bathroom,
all of Ziggy's new friends were there!
"I thought we'd have a pizza party to
celebrate your new home!" said the lady.

Ziggy was so happy.
He was no longer a street dog.

ZiGGY FOUND A HOME!

THE END

but really...just the beginning.

Acknowledgements

I have to start by acknowledging the best pup in the world who inspired this book, my sweet little Ziggy. He makes my life so happy and gives me joy every day.

To all animal rescues, thank you for rescuing amazing dogs like Ziggy and giving them another chance at a great life. I'm thankful for the people who found him on the street and took him to a shelter, as well as, the ones who fostered him before I adopted him.

To my family, thank you for always being my biggest fans and encouraging me with every creative adventure.

Lisha, Courtney and Dani, thank you for your help during the writing process and your great editing skills. I appreciate your expertise.

To my friends and supporters, Bobbie, Shonda, Janna, Elaina and Cassie, I'm grateful for your encouragement and advice along the way.

Finally, Ziggy would like to thank his buddy Bronx for all the fun play dates together and many more to come.

About Amy & Ziggy

Amy Nickerson is a designer, illustrator and photographer living and working in Oklahoma City. She has been actively involved in the OKC design community for the past 11 years. She published her first children's book, Make Friends with Strange Cats, in 2014.

Amy adopted Ziggy in November of 2017. She attended a local pet adoption event, and it was love at first sight. Ziggy was a stray before he was fostered and eventually adopted. He was found wandering around the Plaza district not too far from Amy's home. It said on his bio that he was searching for a tasty slice of pizza, which gave Amy the inspiration for writing this book.

Amy and Ziggy now enjoy going for walks, playing fetch with a tennis ball and, of course, eating pizza!

CPSIA information can be obtained
at www.ICGtesting.com
Printed in the USA
LVHW070808171118
597351LV00001B/1/P